THE GUARDIAN'S CHALLENGE

ORCHARD

MEET ASH AND PIKACHU!

ASH

A Pokémon dreamer who wants to have it all – including becoming a Pokémon Master!

PIKACHU

Ash's First Partner Pokémon and long-time companion!

LOOK OUT FOR THESE POKÉMON

TAPU KOKO

EXEGGUTOR

POPPLIO

TOGEDEMARU

ROCKRUFF

CONTENTS

PART 1: A DAY AT SCHOOL

PART TWO: ALOLA WELCOME

PART THREE: A BIG SURPRISE

PART ONE
A Day at School

CHAPTER ONE

Z-Ring

It was morning on Melemele Island in the Alola region. In the Pokémon School the class were practising their skills with their Pokémon.

Then Professor Kukui walked in, leading Ash and Pikachu.

"Good morning, class,"
the teacher said. "You
remember Ash. He'll be joining
us here at the Pokémon School
for a while!"

"Hi, guys," said Ash happily.
"I'm so glad to be here."

The class all called out greetings, except for an older boy called Kiawe, who looked at Ash through narrowed eyes.

"Is that a Z-Ring?" a boy called Sophocles asked Ash, pointing to Ash's wristband.

"Yes," said Kiawe suspiciously.

"Where did you get that? You didn't take part in the Island Challenge." He rubbed the matching band around his own wrist.

"No," Ash admitted. "Tapu Koko gave it to me."

"You saw the Guardian Pokémon of Melemele Island again?" a girl called Mallow asked in disbelief.

Ash nodded. "Pikachu and I heard Tapu Koko's voice, so we followed it. This band came floating down to us."

The others gaped.

"I've read a lot about Tapu Koko," said a girl called Lillie. "It's believed that the Guardian protects Melemele islanders, but sometimes plays tricks too. Very rarely it also gives gifts to people it likes."

Ash looked at Kiawe's Z-Ring. "Hey, does this mean now I can use Z-Moves like you?" he asked eagerly. Ash had seen Kiawe use his incredible Z-Moves during a Pokémon battle.

"Using Z-Moves is something that should not be taken lightly!" Kiawe snapped.

CHAPTER TWO

Pokémon Science

"Only when a Pokémon and its Trainer's hearts are joined will the Z-Ring turn their feelings into power," Kiawe said fiercely. "But those feelings must be about something more than themselves."

"Like what?" Ash asked.

"Like doing something for the islands, helping Pokémon, or helping other people." Kiawe frowned seriously. "I hope that you realise what a big responsibility this is."

Ash was silent for a minute. Then he gave a nervous smile. "Kiawe, I don't understand very much about Z-Rings or their power, but I do know how special they are. You can count on me to treat them with respect!"

At last, Kiawe's face softened. "Good," he replied.

"OK, class," called Professor Kukui. "It's time for Pokémon Science."

For Science class, Mr Oak was dressed as an Exeggutor. Ash tried not to giggle at the

sight. Next to the teacher stood a real Exeggutor. But it was much bigger than Ash had ever seen before.

"Many Pokémon look different in the Alola region," Mr Oak explained. "For example, Alolan Exeggutor are taller than others.

This is because of the Alolan climate, which is sunny all year around."

"Wow," said Ash, moving closer to get a better look. "That's so interesting. It's even got a tail," he said, reaching for the Exeggutor.

"Wait, Ash!" Lillie called in alarm. "There's something you should know about its tail!"

Ash looked up but, at the same moment, the Exeggutor's tail lashed towards him, sending him flying.

CHAPTER THREE

Alola Plate

Ash landed with a crash on the other side of the room and lay groaning. "Are you OK?" Sophocles called.

"The tail of the Alolan Exeggutor has a mind of its own," Lillie said to Ash.

"You need to approach carefully in case it decides to attack. That's what I was trying to say before."

Ash stood up, wincing and dusting himself off, before giving a sheepish smile.

That evening, Ash was at Professor Kukui's house, where he was staying while he was on Melemele Island. The professor put Ash's dinner down in front of him.

"That looks delicious!"

"It's called an Alola plate. It's a famous dish from this region."

Ash seized his knife and fork and began eating at once, while the professor put another plate in front of Pikachu and his own Rockruff.

As Professor Kukui sat down
next to Ash with his own
dinner, Ash dropped his knife
and fork and announced, "That
was amazing. Thank you!"

"You've finished already?"
the professor asked in disbelief.

Just then his phone rang and he walked away from the table.

Ash sat on the floor, petting Rockruff.

"Professor Kukui here," Ash heard him greeting the caller. "Mmm-hmmm. I see …" The professor lowered his voice and turned away.

Who was he talking to and why didn't he want Ash to know?

PART TWO
Alola Welcome

CHAPTER FOUR

Togedemaru

The next morning Ash and
Pikachu overslept, so they had
to run the whole way to the
Pokémon School.

"Hurry, Pikachu!" Ash
panted. "We might just make it
in time!"

As they sped through the gateway there was a sudden explosion of noise, and streamers fluttered around their faces. Startled, Ash staggered backwards, tripped and landed on the ground.

"Alola surprise!" cried his classmates, as they gathered around him. Ash blinked.

"Did we surprise you?" asked Kiawe, putting out a hand to help pull Ash to his feet.

"You could say that!" Ash replied with a grin.

"We wanted to throw you an Alola welcome party," Mallow said. "And that's just the first surprise!"

"The first?" Ash repeated, confused.

"Yes," said Sophocles. "Next,

Togedemaru and I want to challenge you!"

A smile crept across Ash's face. "A Pokémon battle? You're on!"

Sophocles just grinned. "Follow me," he said.

Sophocles and his Togedemaru led the way further into the school playground … to where two large paddling pools full of balloons waited.

"Balloons?" Ash wondered.

"That's right," Mallow said. "Whichever team pops all their balloons first wins!"

Ash frowned. This wasn't like any Pokémon battle he'd ever taken part in! But then he smiled. "This should be easy!" he declared.

"Ready?" Kiawe shouted at them. "Go!"

CHAPTER FIVE

Lightning Rod

Both teams ran to their pools.
Ash and Pokémon each picked
up a balloon and tried to pop it
with their hands.

"Oof!" Ash said. "This is
harder than I thought."

Finally his first balloon

popped and he looked
up with satisfaction, only
to see Sophocles popping
balloon after balloon against
Togedemaru's spines.

"They're fast!" Ash said to
Pikachu. "How are we going to
beat them?"

"You can do it, Ash!" Mallow called from the sidelines.

"You're allowed to use Pokémon moves," Lillie hinted.

"Really?" Ash asked. "All right, Pikachu — let's pop all the balloons using your Thunderbolt move!"

"Pika …" Pikachu replied, charging up for Thunderbolt.

Sophocles smiled. "Come on, Togedemaru!" he said softly. "This is our chance."

"… chu!" Pikachu yelled, releasing Thunderbolt.

As Ash and Pikachu watched in astonishment, Togedemaru absorbed all the electric energy from Pikachu's attack. Swirling around, it tore through the balloons, popping them in a matter of seconds.

Ash stood rubbing his head.

"What is that?" he asked.

"Togedemaru's Ability is Lightning Rod," Sophocles replied, grinning. "It absorbs lightning bolts with its spines. Then it can release that stored power as a move. Great, huh?"

"That is really cool," Ash had to admit. "Togedemaru is amazing!"

Kiawe laughed. "This is no time to be impressed," he said, gesturing towards the pool as Togedemaru popped the last balloon.

"The winners are Togedemaru and Sophocles!" Mallow announced.

CHAPTER SIX

Popplio

Sophocles swept his Pokémon into the air. "You were amazing!" he said.

Ash smiled, clapping. They had won fair and square.

"Ash?" said a soft voice. Ash turned to see Lana and her

Popplio standing behind him.
"Are you ready for your third
surprise?" she asked shyly. "It's
a challenge against us!"

Ash nodded excitedly
and followed them both over
to the lake.

"In this race, the Pokémon have to first run and then swim," Mallow explained.

Ash and his new friends gathered by the water's edge to cheer Pikachu and Popplio on.

"Ready, get set, go!" Mallow called and the race began.

Pikachu was easily ahead as the two Pokémon raced across land. But once Popplio had dived into the water, it quickly overtook Pikachu.

"Come on, Popplio!" Lana called. "You're almost there!"

With a last burst of speed, Popplio leapt back out of the water and over the finish line!

Ash was amazed.

"Popplio can swim at speeds of twenty-five miles an hour," Lillie said.

"That's so fast!" Ash said, as Pikachu staggered out of the water, looking exhausted.

Ash wrapped Pikachu in a towel. "You did a great job too, Pikachu!" he said.

Kiawe walked over. "Your fourth surprise is competing against me," the older boy said, with a challenging smile.

Ash grinned. "I'm ready!"

PART THREE

A Big Surprise

CHAPTER SEVEN

Tauros Race

For this challenge, Ash and Kiawe raced each other on Tauros, the Will Bull Pokémon.

The race was close. Ash and Kiawe were neck and neck but, as they reached the finish line, Kiawe's Tauros pulled ahead.

"Kiawe wins!" Mallow cried.

"I was so close!" Ash complained.

"You rode well," Kiawe agreed, making Ash smile.

Professor Kukui approached with Rockruff. "Hey, Ash. I'm your fifth surprise. How would you and Pikachu like a Pokémon battle against Rockruff and me?"

"That's the best surprise yet!" Ash said to Professor Kukui. He loved practising his skills in a Pokémon battle.

"But first, it's time for some lunch," Mallow insisted.

Ash opened his mouth to protest – how could he think of eating when there was a Pokémon battle to take part in?

But just then his tummy gave an almighty rumble ...

As Ash was filling his plate with a second helping of another delicious Alola meal, he heard a strange cry.

He spun round to see Tapu Koko – the Pokémon Guardian of Melemele Island. Behind him, Ash heard the others gasp. This was the first time they had seen Tapu Koko.

Ash smiled. "I'm glad to see you again," he said. "I wanted to thank you for the Z-Ring."

But suddenly Tapu Koko seized the hat from Ash's head and flew off.

CHAPTER EIGHT

Tapu Koko

"Hey!" Ash said and began to run after the Guardian Pokémon, the others following.

Tapu Koko came to a stop in a clearing in the forest and faced Ash challengingly.

Lillie tapped Ash's shoulder.

"I've read about this," she said. "Apparently, long ago, Tapu Koko used to challenge Melemele islanders to battle."

Ash's eyes glittered. "OK," he said. "Let's have a battle!"

At once, Tapu Koko leapt up into the air, which began to ripple and spark with energy.

"Ash!" Lillie called. "It's using Electric Terrain. That makes Electric-type Pokémon moves more powerful!"

"That's lucky for us," Ash said, winking at his Electric-

type Pikachu. "Pikachu, use
Thunderbolt!"

"Pikachu!" his Pokémon
roared, sending a Thunderbolt
towards Tapu Koko.

There was a blaze of light,
but then Tapu Koko emerged,
untouched.

"Tapu Koko's just too powerful," Kiawe breathed.

The Guardian Pokémon darted towards Ash and he flinched. But then Tapu Koko gently touched the Z-Ring around Ash's wrist.

"You want me to use Z-Moves?" Ash asked. Tapu Koko just looked at him. "All right," Ash said. "I don't know how, but I'll try!"

Behind him, the others watched nervously.

Ash pulled his arms together

over his head, as he had seen Kiawe do before. He closed his eyes and felt his power connect with Pikachu's.

"Go, Pikachu!" he cried.

CHAPTER NINE

Z-Moves

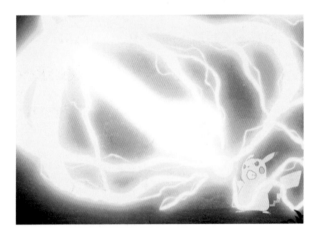

Ash felt a force unlike anything
he had ever experienced,
as Pikachu's Z-Move burst
forward. It sent swirling,
crackling energy speeding
towards Tapu Koko.

The forest shook with the effects of the powerful move and Ash ducked down.

"That's a Z-Move?" Ash said to himself, panting. He looked up to see Tapu Koko emerging from a huge crater.

The Guardian Pokémon paused and nodded once, before flying away.

The others ran up to Ash, cheering.

"That was amazing!" said Mallow. "You and Pikachu are so strong!"

"What happened to the crystal in your Z-Ring?" Kiawe asked.

Ash looked down.

"Oh, no!" he said.

The crystal had shattered.

"That's because you weren't ready to use Z-Moves," Kiawe said sternly. "Because you haven't taken the Island Challenge."

For a moment, Ash felt downcast. Then he smiled with new determination. "All right, I'll take the Island Challenge and learn how to use Z-Moves properly. Will you all help me?"

"Of course!" agreed his new friends.

Once more, Kiawe was the only one who remained silent.

"Come on, Kiawe," Lillie said gently. "Ash needs you."

"Well," the older boy replied. "I suppose I am the only one here who knows how to use Z-Moves …"

The others all cheered and

Ash grinned. He had a feeling that his adventures in Alola had only just begun.

The End

DON'T MISS THESE OTHER OFFICIAL POKÉMON BOOKS